THE SIREN WARS SAGA

ORIGINS OF THE SIREN WARS

prequel novella

by

K.M. Robinson

Origins of the Siren Wars

My skin tingles under the deep rays of the sun as I stretch out on the castle steps. The edges of the water cascade over my fins—a stark contrast to the warm rays of light.

I shiver in delight.

Jarek runs his fingers over my hair, tangling them in my locks as he brushes my tresses. His boots rest near my head and I lazily rest my arm over his feet. I smile up at him, returning his grin before he looks out at the sea.

"That sounds magical, Aila," Jarek remarks in a far-off voice. "I wish I could see that."

"Perhaps one day you will, Jarek," Persephone leans over, resting her head on the prince's shoulder.

"I've known you for four years, Seph, and never once have I been able to swim far enough or hold my breath long enough to visit your realm," he replies sadly. "It's just my luck that I would end up with two such optimistic best friends. I'll never be able to visit you though—at least, not beneath the surface."

"Which is why we come to *you,* our friend," I say, pushing myself upright. I rest a hand on his knee, gently lowering my chin.

"You know I adore your visits," he recovers, offering a smile. His eyes are still sad.

Jarek looks transfixed on something out in the water. When I turn, a ship sails in the distance, so far away that it's a foggy mass embedded in the clouds of the setting sun.

"You girls should probably go home," Jarek sighs. "It will be dark soon and you don't want to get caught during feeding time."

Traveling in the dark doesn't scare mer, but traveling when the sharks make their way in to find their dinner is a terrifying experience.

"We'll be fine, Jarek," Seph tries to convince him. "Just a few more minutes."

"No," he shakes his head. "I must insist that you go. You can come visit me again soon."

He stands to his feet, nearly knocking Persephone and I off balance. The prince retreats up the steps to the landing at the top of the concrete staircase leading to the water. He produces something shiny, holding it up for us before he walks back down the stairs.

"Take this to your grandfather, Aila, as a sign of our respect."

He places a golden ring in my hand encrusted in

pearls. The sunlight glints off it, flaring into my eyes. I run my fingers over the intricate design.

"If you put it on your thumb, it will make it harder to lose," he smirks. "You both have such tiny hands."

"Delicate," Persephone corrects him, making him chuckle.

"Off you go," he nods toward the ocean. "I'll see you ladies again soon."

We wave before slipping off of the steps and dropping into the water. The water surrounding my face, pulling my hair away from my body as I descend into the ocean, is comforting and refreshing.

"I don't like that we can't stay longer," Persephone complains as she locates the midwater squids we brought with us to guide us home in the limited light. Once we reach the dark depths, they will glow a pale moonlight green, illuminating our path as we swim. Of course, we can see without them, but they're comforting to have with us.

"We have to go home sometime, cousin," I remind her. I was always the responsible one among us. "Besides, now we have a mission."

I flick my hand at her, showing off the ring.

"I'm not sure why he gave it to *you*," she grumbles.

"I'm more responsible," I inform her playfully.

"It's probably because you have bigger hands," she shoots back, darting ahead as we swim.

The ring suddenly feels heavier on my finger as I swim to catch up to her, her blue tail glittering in the light from the setting sun. Eventually, she gives up resisting and speaks to me again, chattering the rest of the way home.

Upon arriving, I dart into the palace grotto. The roascea colony floating at the top of the grotto resembles the chandelier from Jarek's palace window. Their long, glowing tentacles sway with the movement of the water.

"Grandfather?" I call, knowing he's somewhere in the palace walls. "Grandfather?"

I find him tucked away in his study, pouring over the rock garden he had built in the shape of the kingdom. He smiles, motioning me inside when he notices me floating in the open entryway.

"Aila," he says softly. "How was your trip to the surface?"

"It was nice, grandfather. Jarek sent something for you."

I wriggle the gold ring off my finger.

"And how is Prince Jarek doing? Is he well?"

"He is," I reply, handing over the gift. "This is a sign of his respect."

My grandfather examines the ring, finally placing it on his right hand.

"Jarek has always been a good boy. He'll make a fine man someday and an even better king."

Persephone would give Grandfather an earful if she heard him call the prince a boy. He's eighteen, as are we, though I understand Grandfather's point more than my cousin would—we're still young, even for our years.

A small school of fish buzzes into the room, darting in and immediately back out when they notice us. The tiniest wave reaches out to me after a moment from the water they displaced by their sudden movements. It feathers over my skin just enough to notice it.

"This was a lovely gesture—I'm impressed he remembered the celebration. Please thank him for me," my grandfather adds. "Actually, perhaps you could take this back to him to give his mother."

He hands a conch shell message. It will whisper the queen's name, directing anyone who finds it to give it to the proper recipient. When she listens to it, it will repeat my grandfather's words only once before fizzling off like foam washing out of the ocean onto the sand.

"I can take it tomorrow," I promise, taking the conch from him. I clutch it to my chest.

"Very good. You should get some rest. It would be wise to deliver it in the morning since we're so busy tomorrow afternoon. It's a little early, but you could use the extra sleep anyway," he sends me off.

Inside my room, I place the note in my jewelry box. The shells encrusting the rectangle are familiar under my palms as I open the lid. The note rests against my hair jewels, waiting for me to wake.

I untangle the hair comb from my locks, having become entwined in my tresses when Jarek ran his finger absentmindedly over them like he might pet one of the dogs I've seen running the palace grounds. A few strands of my hair rip out when I pull it away, but I can remove them from the turquoise comb tomorrow.

I love traveling with my cousin, but it would be nice to have some alone time tomorrow while I swim to the surface. I'll leave before Persephone can wake up.

I float over to my bed and pull the seaweed blanket over my tail, nestling in for the night.

By the time I surface, the sun is over the horizon, dousing the entire world in brilliant shades of pink and orange. The sunlight reflects off of the palace walls, dancing back at me as it twinkles.

The opalescent shine to the outside of the palace amazes me every time I see it—it's more radiant than anything we have under the sea. To be fair, they don't have the coral reefs we have, so I suppose it's almost an even trade.

As I swim closer to the stairs connecting land and sea,

I notice Jarek's head bobbing in the water. He treads in a circle, searching for something.

Suddenly, another person rises out of the water, wrapping their arms around his neck. The girl pulls him close. He chuckles, wrapping his arms around her.

I pause, feeling uncomfortable approaching him while he's with someone.

Why didn't he tell me?

They bob in the water together, slowly spinning in the sunrise. His back is to me when I finally recognize her —Persephone.

She tangles her hands in his hair, drawing him closer. My cousin whispers something to him as they spin slowly, bobbing with the waves.

I splash back in the water when she kisses him, pulling his mouth to hers. Praying the sound of my movements mixed with the splash of the waves against my back, I wait.

Unfortunately, they turn, spotting me against the blue water. Jarek pales when he sees me, but Persephone only freezes for a moment before tipping the prince's head toward her and kissing his lips one more time.

She swims to me, leaving him behind in the waves as if nothing is wrong. Her smile makes me uncomfortable.

"Hi, Aila." She ducks her head under the water, wetting her hair to make it easier to slick back.

"I…" I mumble, blinking back my confusion.

"Why are you here?" she asks sweetly, trying to distract me.

"Grandfather sent a message to the queen," I hold up the conch.

She snatches it from my hand and swims quickly over to Jarek who is still watching us. My cousin hands it to him before darting back to me. She grabs my wrist and drags me under the water.

I look over my shoulder—having no control over my other movements—and see Jarek's feet as he kicks his way back to the shore.

"Persephone, what was that?" I ask when she finally slows as we reach the bed of seaweed near the ocean floor. It waves to us, beckoning us to play.

"Nothing," she claims. "What was grandfather's shell about?"

I truthfully had no idea what he wanted, but that wasn't the point.

"You were kissing Jarek," I try to keep the confusion out of my voice but to no avail.

"Yes," she looks back at me, finally releasing my wrist.

"But Jarek has never been interested in us. After all, mer and humans can never be together," I try to process the situation.

"We can," she announces stubbornly. A lock of her hair floats in front of her face prompting her to angrily brush it back in the water.

"You can...*what?*"

"We can be together—Jarek and I. I'm going to make it happen."

"How?" I stop swimming, putting my hands on my hips. I wish I had added a belt like grandfather's this morning to make me look more powerful and imposing, but at least my *iluse* was striking and fierce with its collection of netting, shells, and pearls on my chest. "You can't grow legs, you know, and he can't breathe underwater."

"We'll see about that," she mutters.

"Seph, you're being ridiculous. It can't happen." I use her family nickname to soften my words.

"We're in love, Aila," she shrieks. For a moment, it looks like she might want to take the words back, but with a slight shake of her head, she banishes those thoughts. She lowers her voice, seething. "We are in love, and we will be together—we'll make it so. You don't have to help me, but you *will* stay out of my way."

She turns, swimming off quickly. I think about going after her, but that would just lead to another fight. I take my time swimming back, not wanting to catch her, but still making sure to be back in time for the festival activities.

The Pearl Ball is held once a year after a week of celebrating. The festivities draw in the entire kingdom, and is not only a large source of income for the merpeople but also offers a well-deserved break.

The first day of the festivities starts slow, opening in the afternoon. For an entire week, mer flood into the palace district, resting their fins with any friend they can find for the duration of the celebration, often times staying at a different home every night.

"Wow, I…*just, wow,*" Troy exclaims as he swims up to me, eyes wide.

I run my hands over my *iluse,* smoothing down the strands of pearls. This had been an outfit I had been saving for months for this occasion.

I try to smile as if nothing is wrong, but I fail miserably. Troy scoops me into his arms, twirling me around.

"You can't look like that and be unhappy," he says playfully. When I don't speak, he adds, "Okay, what is it? Tell me so I can fix it and we can go to the opening festivities."

I pause, debating whether to tell him. Troy and I haven't been dating for very long, and while I trust him, it's still family business.

"I saw Persephone doing something I don't think she should be doing," I admit.

"Making out with Galon?" Troy teases, pulling me closer.

"No."

"Good. I hate that guy." Troy quirks his eyebrow flirtatiously at me. I personally wasn't a fan of Galon and his smugness either.

"She was kissing Jarek," I admit.

"The…prince?" He points up. The water his movement displaces, waves against his dark brown locks, making them sway magnificently. I nod at his reference. "How exactly does she plan on handling that one?"

"You see the problem," I sigh dramatically. "I think I need to tell grandfather—she's convinced they can be together and I just don't see how that could ever work."

"Your grandfather will know what to do," Troy assures me. "We can find him now before the events start."

He tugs at my hand, pulling me toward the festival about to begin in the waterways. His hand is warm and reassuring in mine. Aside from Jarek, Troy is my best guy friend and the perfect fit for me.

Halfway to the open ceremony location, I spot Persephone branching off from the crowd. She waves to a group of her friends, blowing kisses before she swishes her tail, leaving them in a trail of bubbles.

"Did you see—" Troy's words are cut off by my nod. "So we…"

"Are following her. Yes," I reply, changing course.

The sea dances turquoise—my favorite color—as we

quietly follow behind my cousin. Beams of light filter from the surface the higher we get.

Instead of going to the palace, Persephone veers off to the right, taking a route I'm unfamiliar with.

"Do you know where we're going, darling?" Troy asks, pulling me close enough to wrap his arm around my waist. When his wrist hits a strand of pearls, he drops his hand lower.

A cold current chills me to my bones as we swim through it. Troy tries to lend me his warmth, but nothing helps the feel a mer gets from a current.

"I haven't been here before."

Everything around us gets dark. We push forward, following the remnants of the bubbles my cousin leaves in her wake. When we surface, we find ourselves inside a cavern.

The walls glow blue, little streaks of light crawling up the rocks. The water takes on a mystical hue, glowing with the reflection of the spores on the wall.

Persephone's arms rest on the edge of the ground, tail still dangling in the water. She sings into Jarek's ear, using her siren's voice.

Troy turns to look at me, afraid to say anything and risk my cousin hearing us. I pull him under the water to keep our voices from echoing.

"She said they would be together, one way or the other," I whisper. "Troy, I think she's sirening him."

"That's not how we're supposed to use those abilities," Troy counters.

"I know." I glance at my cousin's blue tail, the ends of her long, dark locks floating in the water around her waist. "I don't think Jarek is actually in love with her like she says he is, Troy."

"I don't think so either."

Jarek leans forward, laying down on his stomach to be closer to Persephone. He looks mesmerized by her voice as he leans toward her.

She reaches up, entangling her hand in his. Slowly, she dips their hands into the cool water, bringing it back up a moment later. Seph leans forward singing in his ear a mere inch away.

When she looks toward the water, he smiles at her. Jarek pushes forward, diving into the water while still holding her hand.

Troy and I immediately back up, shooting under the water toward the cavern entrance. We hide behind the walls, only allowing our eyes to peek beyond the rocks.

Jarek and Persephone remain under the surface, bubbles slipping up to where the water meets the air. When she doesn't pull the prince up, I begin to panic. Even Troy grabs a hold of me, worry evident in his nervous fingertips.

Persephone places her lips on Jarek's, breaking them

apart for a kiss. She kisses him over and over as the remaining air in the prince's lungs slips away.

"She thinks her love will help him breathe underwater," I murmur, thinking back to what my cousin had said earlier.

"She's not *magic!*" Troy cries. "We have to do something."

"She's going to kill him," I realize, snapping out of the fog I was in, coming back to my senses.

I dart forward, racing through the water toward the pair. Troy immediately follows, quickly overtaking me with his powerful tail. I silently curse the pearls around my torso for slowing me down.

Troy rips them apart just as I reach them. My hands grasp Seph's shoulders as I wrench her back in the water. Shocked, she doesn't fight me for a moment.

When she does come back to life, it's too late—Troy is already carrying Jarek to the surface. With an incredible show of strength, Troy lifts the man onto the land as my cousin lashes out at me.

I slap, twisting her around and letting go before darting to the surface quickly enough that I propel myself out of the water like a dolphin or a whale and land alongside of Jarek's lifeless body.

"Handle him," Troy directs me, turning back to keep my cousin away while I work.

Once, when I was younger, I watched a child toddle

into the ocean. His distracted tutor reached him long before I did and when I reached the shore, the man was pressing on the child's chest, trying to expel the water from his body. Miraculously, the child came back to life.

I throw my weight against Jarek's chest, though I don't have the leverage I need from a sitting position—I supposed that's at least *one* use for having legs. I beat against him the way the tutor viciously fought against death for the small boy.

After minutes—or a lifetime—Jarek coughs up water. He chokes as he sits up.

"It didn't work," he says sadly.

"What were you thinking?" I chastise him. "You nearly died, Jarek."

"She said it would work."

"Well, it didn't!" I can't help my exasperation. "That was foolish and careless. What would your mother do if you died? What would she do if you just *left and lived under the sea*? Jarek, you can't do things like this."

"But I love her," he protests.

"No, you don't. She sirened you. Her singing convinced you to do something you wouldn't ordinarily do—our voices have the power to change minds and fates."

"I don't believe that." He tries crossing his arms, only to trigger another coughing fit.

"Lay back down," I direct him.

"I don't want to," he says stubbornly.

"*Good*. Now pay attention." I start singing, letting my siren-call free. After a moment, he leans back, lying against the cold, harsh rocks of the cavern floor. "Let me remind you that only a moment ago, you refused to lay down, and yet, here you are—laying down."

"It's because I *sirened* you, Jarek," I conclude.

"This is madness," he says, eyes shifting to look at me while he remains on the cavern floor.

"I told you."

Troy and Persephone pop out of the water, breaking the surface loudly as they struggle. I slip into the water.

"Go inside, Jarek. Don't come back to this cavern—ever. I'll come back to you when it's safe, but for coral's sake, don't go near the water alone until I can talk some sense into her."

Jarek looks bewildered as he stares at the mermaid and merman struggling near the mouth of the cavern. They fight like two fish thrown in a bucket, struggling to survive. Their splashing creates large waves that rock me in the water, slamming my stomach into the side of the rocks.

"Jarek, please," I beg for his attention. He tears his eyes off them and focuses on me. "If you go near her and she sirens you again, you could drown—she nearly killed you this time. Please, Jarek, I beg you—don't go near the water alone."

I pull my hands away from the side of the ledge.

"I'll be back. Just go!"

Jarek stands, rushing away from the cavern. I turn, diving under the water toward my cousin, fury running through my veins.

I catch her by the tail and drag her away from the cavern—my strength surprising even me. She tries to pull away, but it only serves to jerk my arm back and forth as I move her backward under the waves. Troy catches up to me, wrapping his hand around her tail just above mine, lending me his strength should I need it to pull her.

Persephone screams the entire way to the seafloor, but we don't stop until we reach the coral that surrounds the land kingdom, indicating where the swimmers should turn around.

"What were you thinking?" I scream at my cousin. "You drowned him! He *died*, Persephone!"

"He didn't," she counters, still trying to pull away from us. "He would have breathed, I know it."

"No, he wouldn't have. He's a *human*—he's not made to live under the water."

"Persephone, you're playing a very dangerous game here," Troy warns her. "Your grandfather would never approve."

"He understands *love*," she growls at us, looking like a shark that has spotted its prey.

"I've had enough." I latch on to her wrist. Troy immediately matches me, turning Seph around in the water to swim the same way we are. We force her along. She bucks like an eel, trying to slither away from us.

When we arrive, the festivities are in full splash. Mer fill the waterways, adorned in pearls and fancy *iluses*, belts, chestplates and shoulder armor.

We go immediately to the palace where we find Persephone's mother.

"What is going on here?" she looks horrified at us, pulling her daughter along as if we are a jellyfish pulling its dinner toward itself.

"She tried to drown Prince Jarek," I announce indignantly.

"Excuse me?" my aunt snorts.

"She sirened him because she's in love with him and he drowned. I barely managed to save him."

"I did no such thing," Persephone protests, struggling against us. Her tail crashes into mine and I worry I might have lost a few scales.

My aunt swims to us, grabbing her daughter's hand away from Troy. She turns, dragging Seph behind her, locking them in her daughter's room.

"Go get my grandfather," I turn to Troy. "I'll wait here."

I set up vigil outside my cousin's door. I can't make out what my aunt and Persephone are saying, but it sounds harsh. I feel terrible that my cousin is suffering, but it's better to get it over with now before it becomes harder to handle—and more dangerous.

"Gather your cousins," Grandfather says after I explain the situation. "We'll talk in the grotto."

I suddenly wish Troy had been able to stay by my side through the lecture, but only the cousins were allowed to participate in the discussion. Our parents hovered near the rocky walls while the younger generation floats closer to our patriarch.

Persephone's mother argues with Grandfather, raging about Persephone's right to siren a man she loves—I hadn't anticipated her taking her daughter's side.

"We were not meant to use our gifts to hurt others, daughter," Grandfather says dangerously. His tail flicks behind him, showing his rage. "Our songs are only meant to help and guide. We have always used our voices to protect."

"We all understand our duty and agreement to help the humans," my aunt snaps. "We've all honored that. It's nearly a rite of passage for mer to guide a ship through a storm or locate and rescue a drowning human."

She places her hands on her hips, glaring.

"Mer have done a great deal for the humans—*more*

than they've done for us—and there is no reason to take this from Persephone."

Persephone weeps near the side of the room. My cousins all keep their distance until they decide if it's safe to associate with her or not in front of Grandfather.

"She will never have any place here. Your title will be passed to your eldest, and then to her eldest." My aunt glares at my older cousin, Kailania. "Persephone could have her own title and kingdom and it wouldn't affect anyone here—in fact, it would only make the human-mer bond stronger."

"How do you expect her to live like that—her in the sea and him on land—what kind of a *life* is that?" my grandfather challenges. He turns on Persephone. "You will not see the prince again. You both were made for so much more. It may not be fair, but it is the way that it is."

"Father!" my aunt shouts.

"This violates the human-mer agreement. We've honored it for one hundred years, daughter," my grandfather rages, voice filling the grotto. "Do you remember what happened when humans first discovered merpeople? They captured the mer in their nets and strung their bodies up on their ships, taking them back to land as trophies, even giving their corpses as rewards. Marcelline had to risk her life to go to the humans, convincing them that we were more valuable as an alliance than an enemy—she saved our people from certain death as the humans made it their mission to pull us from the sea."

"And if you'll recall," my aunt sneers, "that started with sireny too—that's how Marcelline convinced them to sign the agreement. It wasn't by her wonderful words or brilliant strategy. She failed to convince the king not to destroy us, so she sang to him and changed his mind."

"And we haven't used our sireny on humans since for anything other than to protect them out on the seas," Grandfather concludes. "Marcelline may not have put it in the agreement with King Leon, but it was always a part of the mer's promise—we would not harm them."

"*The tides are changing*, Father."

"Not as long as I reign," he bellows. "You will follow my orders."

Persephone cries out, racing out of the grotto. Grandfather's nostrils flare as he motions to one of my uncles by the door.

"Follow her," he turns on my aunt, anger burning in his eyes. "*You* will stay."

Several of the uncles follow Persephone out. The rest of us hover in place, afraid to move. The arguing continues for several hours.

I finally sink to the floor, leaning against the walls as the parents fight with Grandfather and my aunt, Chantay. I'm surprised at which side some of them take. My cousins and I listen quietly.

My fingers float up, dancing in a school of tiny fish absent-mindedly when the uncles race back in. They look frantic as they fill the room.

"Persephone went to the surface," one proclaims.

"She went to the prince. His mother was there—" another adds.

"She tried to siren him from the shores and when he ran to the water, the queen's men stopped him."

"Barely," my eldest uncle mumbles.

"The queen and her guards rushed to the water, while her men held back the prince," my father exclaimed. "Persephone challenged her wishes and refused to leave without the prince.

"When she moved to the shore and sirened him again, the queen had her shackled to the land and demanded we bring you to her."

My aunt races out of the room, not staying to hear more. Grandfather starts to follow but holds back long enough to hear the rest of the information from my uncles on the situation.

He commands us to wait as he swims off with my parents, aunts and uncles to rescue Persephone and make peace with the queen and her son.

The next few hours are the hardest of my life.

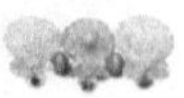

"It will be okay," Troy tries to soothe me, combing my hair.

My shell crown sits on the table next to us as he pulls a bone comb through my silver locks. I lean back into his skilled hands as he works his magic on my hair.

In the corner of the room, an octopus sits, watching the scene. I've always been fond of the pink thing that lurks in the palace, though I could do without the occasional brush of its tentacle.

"I'm sure they'll be back soon," Kailania remarks for the tenth time. Her fingers slip nervously to her crown adorned in gems and crystals. Pearls accent each rock for the festivities.

"This is a fabulous way to celebrate the opening ceremonies," one of the girls mumbles.

"Should we take over with the parade?" I ask, realizing that no one has been overseeing the events.

"I'll go if they aren't back soon," Kailania says in a confident voice. She may not be strong-willed, but when it comes to her royal duties, she holds true.

Troy's movements are comforting. One of my cousins eyes him with jealousy. Several of our companions occupy the room with us, though none of the newer relationships are welcome yet until we get to know them. Troy is particularly good-looking compared to the others, despite them being some of the most eligible mermen in the kingdom.

"Did you find her?" Kailania asks, swimming up quickly from her seat.

One of my uncles cradles his arm in his hand. My mother looks worse for the wear. My youngest aunt—the peacemaker—has a nasty scratch across her cheek.

"We found her," Grandfather confirms. "I convinced the queen to leave Persephone in my custody and we had planned on discussing how to handle the situation."

He pauses, deciding how to continue.

"Send the messengers," he turns to my uncles. "Send them into every kingdom under the sea—no one is to surface until this is resolved.

"The mer are not to leave the depths, or they risk their lives and our treaty and future safety."

Something terrible has happened.

"Grandfather?" I push away from my seat, nearly knocking Troy's hand away.

"Your aunt made a terrible decision," my grandfather says, voice laced in sadness. "When the queen wouldn't relinquish Persephone to anyone but me, your aunt swam away. The queen thought it was to find me and bring me to the surface faster, but instead, she swam to the coves where the fisherman like to work."

I hold my breath, already knowing where this was going. Squeezing my eyes shut, I mourn the loss of my friend and our lives as we know them.

"She sirened a ship, luring them onto the rocks. The

men all drowned and the ship was lost." He hangs his head in shame. "She broke the treaty and now we're all in danger.

"Everyone must stay under the sea until I can fix this with the queen."

"The people," my uncle interjects, "are angry. They already know what has happened. Many of them are hunting us in revenge."

Just like that, all of Marcelline's work has been undone.

"Gather everyone. The festivities are hereby canceled. I need to address the people and tell them what has happened." Grandfather motions for his children to set everything up for the announcement. "There's something else you should know.

"Before word of the sunken ship reached the palace, your aunt arrived. She took Persephone, claiming she was bringing her home while I tried to calm the queen.

"Several of us went with them to see that they made it back safely, but they attacked us. We don't know where Chantay or Persephone are, nor what they plan to do."

That would explain my mother's appearance.

Grandfather motions us forward, and we follow him to the courtyard to address the people.

At first, everyone sides with my aunt and Persephone, horrified over the thought of one of us being shackled to land. My grandfather calms them down, explaining it was both Persephone and Chantay who were in the wrong for breaking the agreement—the queen's actions, while harsh, were only done to prevent my cousin from doing any more damage until our leader could address the situation.

Grandfather pleaded with everyone to stay inside the festival limits for the time being, urging them that it was safer when we were closer together. Eventually, we all wandered back to where we would spend the night.

"I have something to show you," Troy smirks, tugging at my wrist.

"It's late, Troy," I gently pull back.

"All the better," he teases, swimming away from me. "Coming?"

I sigh, following after him. Kailania and Ebba follow after their mermen as well, working together to get us out of our heads. The mermen guide us away from the palace, into the dark waters.

Several midwater squids join us, illuminating our path with their glowing bodies.

"Where are we going?" I ask.

"To the Scur Caverns," he grins. We all start to swim faster at the thought of the glowing underwater cave that mimics the storm clouds above the surface. It's a beautiful, adventurous location that isn't easy to reach—romantic too.

In the distance, something glows. It's muted and dull, but it's there. Knowing we need to investigate, we veer off course, swimming toward the light as we douse our own, concealing the creatures swimming with us.

Persephone and her mother swim just far enough below the surface that they can't be easily seen by men on ships.

"This can't be good," Troy murmurs.

Kailania dives to the ocean floor, grabbing at the first conch she sees. She whispers into it before attaching it to her squid.

"Home," she commands it. The creature takes off into the murky waters to deliver her message to our grandfather. "Let's go."

We follow the mermaids toward the land.

"Aila, if it comes to it, you may need to be the one to negotiate with Jarek and the queen—they know you far better than they know me," Kailania says as we race toward them. Catching up to my aunt and cousin seems impossible at this distance.

"It will all be okay," I try to assure her as much as

myself. Troy's hand gently finds my waist, lending me his support.

On the surface, guards hold vigil along the water's edge. As we approach, we find them jumping into the sea, drowning.

Persephone and Chantay call to them, ending their lives one at a time until only a few remain. The men run inside, hoping to find reinforcements. Instead, the queen and Jarek run out to investigate.

We reach them just in time to hear Jarek rebuff Persephone's final advances. When he denies her, she sings to him, calling him into her arms.

"No," I scream, trying to break the trance. "Jarek!"

My shrieks are to no avail. Jarek throws himself into the sea, swimming to my cousin. When he reaches her—his mother still screaming from the shore—Persephone drags him under the water.

I dive, the bodies of the dead guards cloud my way like a bloom of jellyfish. I dart around them, knowing they cannot be saved.

"Let him go, Persephone," I shout, pummeling into her. She keeps her grip.

"They tried to hurt me, Aila. They need to be stopped."

"They shackled you so you wouldn't hurt anyone," I counter.

"The queen would have killed me," Seph shouts.

"Like you're doing to Jarek?" I pull on his arm, desperately trying to free him and take him to the surface for air.

"He turned on me," my cousin informs me.

"And you're turning on everyone. Seph, this is ridiculous!" I cry. "You broke the treaty. It will be a miracle if we can repair the damage you've caused."

"We don't need to repair anything," she informs me, trying to take Jarek deeper into the water. "We won't need to worry about the humans at all—they'll obey our every command."

"We're not going to siren them," I argue. "We've had an agreement for one hundred years—"

"Yes, and now our oppression is over," she looks at me with wild eyes.

I've had enough.

I scratch at her, drawing blood. In the dark of night in the shallow depths of the water near the palace, predators will surely be nearby. She has two choices—sacrifice herself and take the prince down with her, or release him and survive.

Ebba appears next to me, scratching at Persephone as she attempts to pull her away. Seph loses her grip on the prince and I drag him up.

We burst through the surface, the cool night air stinging my cheeks. Ebba pops out of the water, grabbing Jarek's other arm. We pull him toward the shore.

Kailania shouts with the queen, trying to calm her, but with her son out of her sight, the queen's fear turns to rage. Troy and the others try to help, searching the sinking bodies for possible survivors—though we all know there are none. The mermen drag the bodies to the shore to give their families some comfort.

The moon sparkles off the surface of the water. It would have been even lovelier had the water not been so choppy from the rescue efforts. The pale silver glow matches my hair as I force Jarek's lifeless body toward the shore.

"Is he dead?" Ebba asks, panic seething out through her words.

"I don't know," I respond, unsure if he can be saved a second time.

Kailania screams in terror, splashing back in the water.

"Harpoons, get down," she warns us, diving under the water.

"Go," I command Ebba. She hesitates before diving under the water.

With only a few feet to go, I push my tail with all of the strength I have. I feel like everything in me is going to break. I push Jarek up, slamming his chest into the land.

I can't push him up any higher, so I stabilize him before leaping up to sit on the steps. Pulling does little good.

"Your majesty," I shriek, trying to get the queen's attention. She notices me, running toward us.

Her men notice too.

A harpoon flies in my direction, sinking into the water a few feet away.

"Don't hit Jarek," the queen wails, lifting her skirt to run. She trips, stumbling in the darkness.

Another weapon flies at me—this one dangerously close.

A guard runs at me, overtaking the queen. My eyes grow wide for he has no intention of doing anything other then skewering the mermaid who killed his prince.

"I'm sorry," I whisper to Jarek before throwing myself off the steps I had spent the last few years of my life on.

I knew the moment I touched the water that I would never see those steps again.

"Aila," Troy appears, frightening me. He wraps himself around me, forcing me away from the palace.

Arrows dive into the water, having been shot from the highest towers and walls of Jarek's palace. One slices into Troy's arm, ripping his flesh open.

I scream, but it only pushes Troy to move faster, propelling us away from harm. My hair floats straight out behind me, and I can feel it resisting against the water, slowing us down. I'm suddenly grateful I replaced my pearl *iluse* for a more practical one.

I glance back over my shoulder as Troy guides me.

The arrows sink in the distance until we're far enough away that I can't make out their skinny figures in the depths.

"Are you okay?" I croak out, trying to see Troy's injury.

"I'm fine," he replies quickly, out of breath. "Are you hurt?"

"I don't think so," I try to examine myself, but our speed and my adrenaline prevent me from taking a proper assessment.

"Where are Chantay and Persephone?" Kailania asks, her beau wrapped around her waist.

"I don't know," I reply as Troy finally slows.

"We need to find grandfather," Ebba insists, swimming back toward us—her merman clearly having pulled her away before Kailania and I escaped. I am grateful to him for protecting her when we couldn't.

"Did Jarek live?" Kailania inquires. She looks as though her own life were the one in question.

"I don't know," I can feel the tears stinging my eyes. "I had to leave him."

Kailania nods, her moves deep and heavy.

"This changes everything," she reminds us.

"Girls," grandfather's voice carries to us as he shouts.

We all spin toward the noise, beating our tails against the water to reach him faster. We crash into him at the same time, knocking him back. He waits for us to explain everything. A collection of mer surround us, floating in the water with the glowing squids.

"I have to go," Grandfather murmurs, pulling us off of him as we protest. "I have to try to fix this."

He takes several of his most fierce mermen with him, swimming for the queen's palace to investigate and try to open a dialogue with the humans.

I fear for his safety.

The depths are quiet as we wait for grandfather to return home.

Light sparkles off the floor of the living quarters, filtering in from the hole in the ceiling. It dances in waves as I focus on it, trying to relieve my worry.

A turtle silently slips into the room, hovering over our heads as he explores. It turns, exposing its belly to me as it glides across the space over my head.

Jarek once told me the only creatures allowed inside his palace were dogs and cats, though sometimes mice got in. Everything else—like the majestic horse I saw him riding once—lived outside.

To me, that seems so strange, as all of our creatures are free to roam where they like. Fish and seahorses frequent the palace. Starfish take up residence in almost every corner. While larger creatures, like sharks and whales can't get in, even the occasional curious dolphin makes an appearance outside my room.

"He's alive," I murmur. "He has to be."

"What?" Ebba asks, pulling her head from my shoulder.

"Nothing," I turn, stroking her hair. "I was just mumbling."

"You think grandfather is all right, don't you?" she asks, allowing herself to float up several inches.

"I'm sure he's fine," I assure her. She puts her head back on my shoulder.

Another hour passes before Grandfather returns.

"The prince is alive," he informs us. I shudder, astonished that he lived a second time. "We, however, cannot stay here.

"The humans are bent on revenge. We cannot hand Persephone and Chantay over to them, and now their sailors are coming after us with a vengeance.

"I don't know where Chantay and Persephone are, but we will protect them from the humans' wrath. We will not hand them over.

"Now, we must protect the rest of our community."

"For many years we've had outliers in the mer community," he begins. "Some have chosen to forgo the ways of the mer, turning to sireny and mercilessness to get what they wanted.

"Those mer were found and dealt with," he continues. "It is with heavy heart that I must inform you that today, my own daughter and granddaughter have chosen to take everything away from the mer community.

"The human prince is alive—barely—thanks to Princess Aila," he motions to me as I hang my head. I'm so grateful that my friend is alive, but I know I shall never see him again. "The treaty protecting humans and mer has been broken.

"With this shattering of the agreement our ancestors made one hundred years ago, our ties to the human world have been dissolved," he looks out at the crowd. "We must leave this place and never return."

The crowd's murmur rises up—fear, agony, remorse, and anger enveloping the collection.

"It is no longer safe," my grandfather insists. "While they have never been to our kingdom, they know enough to find it when the time is right. We cannot stay."

The crowd shifts, unsure of how to respond to this sentence.

"I know some of you are against the outlaw of sireny in any case except when it is necessary for survival. For those of you who take that stand, there is no room in this community for you.

"Get your things and leave immediately," he

concludes. "There is no place for you with us in the new kingdom district.

"If you insist on living this way, we wish you all the best and pray that you survive the humans' wrath when they discover you. From this day forward, we will no longer accept you as one of our own, nor will we be there to support you in your time of need.

"Make up your mind now, for if you leave, you will never be welcomed into the community again, and if you stay, you will live under our laws for the rest of your days."

A group of mer cautiously rises up, turning their backs on our people—more than I expected. They form a collection at the back of the group before swimming away to collect their things and move on.

"From this day forward, we will live quietly in the depths. We will avoid humans at all costs. Sireny is only to be used in extreme cases of survival and any *intentional* interaction with the humans is punishable. You do not want to suffer those consequences—they may be as extreme as refusing you access to our people if you put us in danger."

He finishes with a speech full of encouraging words, giving the merpeople hope, despite the circumstances. Even I—having lost my best friend, my home, and nearly my life—feel ready to move forward and take the next stroke toward the future.

Grandfather finds me in my room as I'm packing my things for the journey. He knocks gently before swimming in.

"Don't get any ideas about going back to the surface, Aila," he cautions me. "Even if you go, Jarek will never be by the sea again—his mother has moved him to another palace somewhere on land for his safety."

"I wouldn't, Grandfather. I know it isn't safe."

I place my crowns in a chest, packing my *iluses* around them for protection during the move. My fingers fall over a strand of pearls I had planned on wearing for tonight's concert.

He notices me lingering on the piece.

"We'll bring all of our traditions with us, my Aila," he says, placing a hand on my shoulder. He runs a finger through my hair, trying to comfort me.

"You've never been to the palace in Scylla before. I think you'll like it there—it has even better lighting than this place," he offers. It was hard to picture somewhere more magical than my childhood home. "You know I just want you to be safe."

"Of course, Grandfather," I fly to his defense. "You're doing the right thing."

"I'm sorry you got dragged into this mess, Aila. It

wasn't fair for Persephone and Chantay to put us in this position."

"No, it wasn't" I reply sadly, turning back to my packing. "We'll be okay."

I scoop up my pile of conch shells that I kept with messages from my parents, friends, and Troy, and place them in my trunk. Grandfather eyes my crowns.

"That one was always my favorite on you," he points to the gold and coral colored crown, encrusted with shells and crystals. "It matches your tail so perfectly."

He sighs.

"We didn't get close to the palace, Aila. We tried, but we found several conch shells the queen left us on the way—that's how we knew what was happening," he waits a moment. "I tried. I'm so sorry."

He swims away, leaving me to finish collecting my things.

The Scylla palace is everything grandfather promised and more—even the water is warmer. A bloom of jellyfish decorates every room and grotto inside the palace walls.

A giant starfish the size of my forearm sits in the corner of my room when I arrive. An octopus scurries off my bed, clearly unhappy with the intrusion.

Several mermen help bring in my trunks, setting them

on the sand. I quickly unpack, wanting to use my first day to explore with Troy.

"Princess," one of the mermen says at my door, carrying in a small box for me. "Princess Kailania requested you join her in the grotto."

I close my treasure chests, covering up my crowns and *iluses* as I thank him. Swimming through the palace, I duck around corners until I locate the grotto—it will take a few days to get used to the layout of the palace.

Kailania looks up as I enter, worry clouding her eyes —I wasn't expecting this expression.

"What?"

Grandfather swims out of the corner of the room, holding his hand open to me. A conch shell sits in his palm.

"This was delivered for you," he holds it out to me. "It's from Persephone."

I swallow, terrified to take the shell and listen to her message. Perhaps she is sorry and wants to come to the palace. Maybe she is inquiring about Jarek's well-being and thinks that because of our friendship, I will have an answer and be willing to share it with her.

I lift the shell to my ear, closing my eyes as the sound swirls around the inside of the shell.

"I know what you did," she hisses through the shell. "I know you sabotaged me—you sirened him first. I understand it all now."

I want to pull the shell from my ear but I know I only get to hear the message once.

"You will pay for what you've done to me and my mother, Aila. You stole the man I loved, banished me from my rightful place with our family, and turned me into a villain.

"You will never be safe, Aila. The world has turned against you and so have I. You should be terrified of the humans, but you should be more worried about me—I'm the greatest siren the world has ever seen—I proved that when I sirened Jarek away from you after you cast your song on him—and I will turn the human world against *you* if it's the last thing I do."

Her words die off, fading into sea foam fizzling on the sand.

My family's faces pale when I tell them of my cousin's words.

"She plans to turn the humans against us even more than she already has," my grandfather whispers in disbelief. "How did I go so wrong?"

"I'm sure Chantay is in on this," my mother mutters, flicking her hand to wave off a small school of fish swimming in her direction. They scatter at her movement.

"We need to protect Aila," Grandfather says. A jolt of electricity runs through me as if I had accidentally brushed against a jellyfish when the thought hits me.

"Troy!"

They all look at me.

"I took Jarek from her—" I don't even finish my sentence before the uncles are swimming away to find him for me.

I wait impatiently as they search for him. It takes longer than normal because they have to locate where his family once lived in Scylla.

"He will be okay, I'm sure of it." Kailania brushes her fingers through my hair quickly. Her frantic movements might suggest otherwise.

"Ships have been spotted in areas the humans have always stayed out of," one of my aunts announces, swimming into the room. "The scouts are back and it doesn't look good."

I'm positive it will be another hundred years before my kind sees the surface again.

"Aila," Troy rushes to me, ignoring the rest of the room. He throws his arms around me, pulling me close. "What happened?"

I quickly explain Persephone's threats, earning myself a look of horror. He spins us around to face my family.

"She will be protected," Grandfather cuts him off. "I understand your worry, my boy, but she will be under the best care possible."

"We'll be baiting the sharks, surrounding the easiest places to enter the kingdom. We'll teach them where to hunt so that they also protect us," my mother explains, clearly having thought this through. "They won't leave an area with an easy food source—we'll provide them with enough motivation to stay, and no one will want to face them to get to us."

"The other entryways are harder to access. It won't be easy for anyone—mer or human—to reach us here once we're done," Grandfather concludes. "And the coral reefs will do the rest."

Grandfather sends mer to see to the sharks, putting their plan into action immediately. We spend the rest of the day working on a plan to keep me safe and unpack the palace.

That night, Troy insists on sleeping outside my door.

Troy leaves early the next morning, long before the cuddlefish have gone to bed for the morning. I comb my hair, not knowing what else to do now that I'm on restriction.

"Princess," a merman hovers in front of my door. "A conch was delivered for you. It's from Princess Ebba."

Conch shells whisper the name of the recipient until it is delivered, but the sender's voice can often be identified if the person who finds it has met them before.

"I'm trapped," Ebba cries. "I'm in a cavern."

She quickly details the location, begging for help.

"Aila, it's Persephone—she says to come alone or she'll take my fins." Ebba sobs into the conch shell. Without her fins, she can't swim—it's one of the worst fates a mermaid can suffer.

Sneaking out of the palace takes a tremendous amount of work. Thankfully, a giant sea turtle glides by the palace walls just as I peek around the corner. I hide behind its shell as it swims away, blocking me from view of the mer guards outside my new home.

When I finally depart from my slow-moving ride, I swim as quickly as I dare toward the location Ebba described. Finding my way around in new surroundings isn't easy, but I quickly discover that Persephone has left signs for me along the way.

She waits outside the cavern with Ebba, her hands tied behind her back. Several strands of seaweed cover Ebba's mouth, preventing her from calling out to me.

Next to her rests a long chain extending to the surface —an anchor.

"We've been inside waiting for you this whole time," Persephone informs me, a sharp shell knife to Ebba's throat. She darts her gaze up to avoid removing her hands from their control over the pink-haired girl. "They're looking for us."

"I'm here, Seph. Let Ebba go."

She pushes our cousin back toward the cavern.

"Now be a good mermaid and stay put. Someone will

be along to help you in a bit." She pats Ebba on the head. Obviously, she still cares about her, but she's also willing to use her to hurt me.

Persephone guides Ebba into the cavern as I swim close. A moment passes with no movement.

"Can't we just talk about this?" I beg, steering clear of the metal weight holding the boat at bay.

"No," she yells, launching herself out of the dark mouth of the cave.

In her hands, she holds a net. Not realizing it was coming, I didn't have time to move. My hands work quickly to rip it off of my body, tail trashing to set myself free.

"They want a mermaid head—any head will do. Those men up there are looking for me, but they don't know the difference between one mermaid and another. I watched them gut a fish half your size and throw it back in the water almost a league from here."

"Persephone!" I struggle against my captor as she pushes me to the ocean floor.

"Actually, you have good timing," she says, pointing up. "Here comes their net."

Once it settles in the water, she drags me up. I try swimming away, but my tail is so constricted by the net, that I can barely move, much less escape.

We're mere inches from the fishermen's net when I find myself floating, falling away from near-capture.

Kailania wrestles with Persephone above me in the water.

The moment I hit the ocean floor, I wriggle myself around, trying to get the net undone. Miraculously, a shell lies on the seafloor.

I beat it against the sand, but it doesn't break. My last resort is snapping it with my hands. I push so hard, I think I might break every bone in my fingers before the shell will snap.

Kailania is pushed dangerously close to the net above me. With a final snap, I break the shell in two, slicing my hand open in the process. It stings as I use the jagged edge of the shell to cut the ropes around me just enough to escape.

My eldest cousin tips Persephone into the net as she tries to swing herself away from it just as the net starts to rise out of the water. Persephone's face is pure terror as she screams for help.

Kailania freezes, processing what is happening. We're banned from helping the mer that left the community… but she's also our dear cousin, and no matter what she has done, we love her.

"Aila!" Kailania screams as I dart back to the ocean floor.

I scoop up the broken shell pieces and race as quickly as I can to the net entrapping Persephone, my own net over my arm. I pass off one half of the broken shell, transferring the net to my non-dominant arm as I saw at the ropes.

"Faster," I warn Kailania. Glancing up, I can see we only have seconds left to spare my cousin from certain death.

The moment she is free, Persephone tries to escape. Kailania brings her shell down on Seph's temple, knocking her out. She sinks quietly to the ocean floor

"Get her in the net," Kailania murmurs, racing toward the sandy bottom of our kingdom.

We tie her up. I float over her as my older cousin rushes into the cavern to get Ebba—she hadn't realized the girl was there when she rescued me.

Kailania had heard from the man who delivered the conch to me that I had received a shell message from Ebba. When she couldn't locate either of us, she figured out what had happened and had come after me. She spotted me from the palace just as I separated from the giant sea turtle and had trailed me the entire way.

Ebba had been knocked out the moment Persephone had pushed her into the cave, but she woke up long before Seph did. Together, the three of us dragged Persephone back to the palace.

Half of the kingdom is looking for us by the time we

return. The mermen take Persephone's bucking body from us, carrying her netting back to the palace.

"Granddaughter, you will answer for your crimes. You will never again leave this palace. Take her to the cells." Our grandfather makes a sweeping motion, summoning his mermen to take her away. "You are my granddaughter, so we will show you mercy, but you will never again see the outside of your cell. *I so proclaim it.*"

"What will we do about Aunt Chantay, Grandfather?" Kailania asks, swimming across the room once Persephone has been taken away.

"I fear we will never find her, nor will she stop trying to get to Persephone.

"You are safe, my dear ones," he looks around at us. "I promise you that. Chantay will not be able to enter our kingdom, but I cannot stop her from trying to destroy the human world and perpetuate the problem between human and mer."

He looks striking as the light filters down from the ceiling, bits of sand floating in the water like stars in the night sky about the surface. His shoulder armor adds a fierce touch to his presence. I have every confidence that my grandfather will protect us.

"The war, my dears, *has just begun.*"

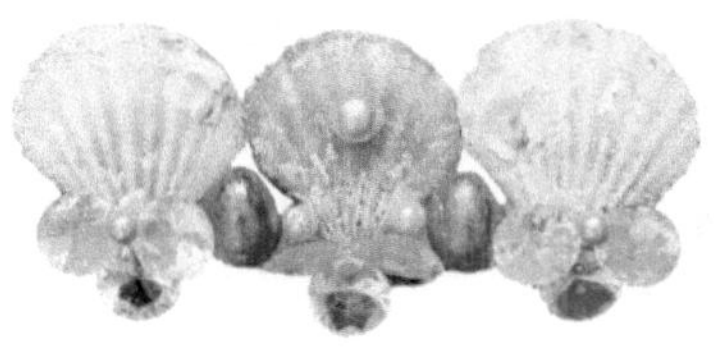

Acknowledgements

Origins of the Siren was originally created to be part of the Of The Deep Mermaid Anthology and was actually the first part of the Siren Wars Saga that I wrote before I started the main series.

I knew I wanted that background information before I jumped into Celena's story and being able to meet Aila has been such a joy for me. I've received so much good feedback on Aila's tale (and tail) over these past few months and I couldn't be more grateful!

Special thanks to Elissa, Jess, and Yentl for all their help with Aila's story.

Thanks to Alexis and Madeline for their stunning drawings of Aila, Persephone, and Jarek for the anthology—you ladies made my babies come to life!

And thank you to my fabulous readers! You've fallen in love with the mermaids and mermen (and sirens… yeah, I see you going after the bad boys…) in my series and it means the world to me! I can't wait for you to see what is next!

If you're totally loving on the series, reach out and email or direct message me—I love hearing from you and talking about my characters! Can't wait to chat!

Stay inspired!

-K.M. Robinson

THE SIREN WARS

War has hovered around the kingdom of Scylla for generations ever since the original sirens left the mer collection generations ago after nearly drowning the human prince. Over the years, select mermaids from the royal bloodline have been trained as spies to work for the reigning kings and queens, keeping the collection safe from sirens and humans.

Celena and her partner, Merrick, work covertly for the royals—not even her twin brother knows. When they discover the sirens have broken through the barriers the mer set up to keep the sirens out, Celena and her friends must race to the old kingdom of Metten to stop them from starting a war within their borders.

When she's dragged to the surface, Celena realizes that the war above the waters is as deadly as the one below the waves—and sacrificing herself may be the only way to protect her family.

The Siren Wars have only just begun.

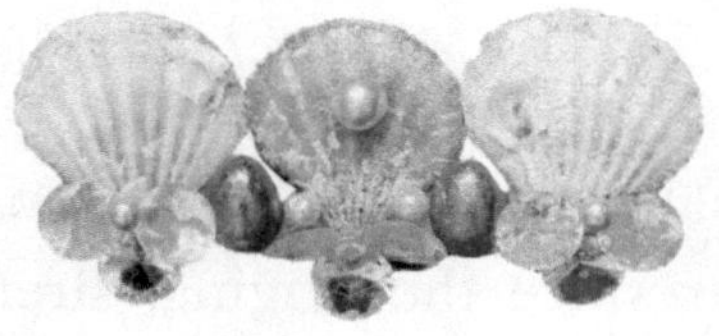

Get your copy at
sirenwarsinfo.kmrobinsonbooks.com

Read the first chapter on the next page!

THE SIREN WARS-CHAPTER 1

A WELL-PLACED ACCUSATION—EVEN A SMALL, insignificant one—has the power to change the tides and start a war.

This is something I've grown up learning.

My kind have always been careful with our words… we have to be. For the last one hundred years, we've had to fight against the actions of one mermaid. Well, to be fair, one mermaid, her mother, and a group of followers, but that's just semantics. For a hundred years before that, we had to be careful too—we had an agreement with the humans.

"Are you intentionally trying to look like that?" I ask, flicking my tail flirtatiously.

"Like what, Celena?" Merrick glances up from where

he's working on the sea floor against a rock, his brow low.

"Brooding," I reply.

His face lights up, realizing that he has been caught.

"Sorry, Len," he uses his pet name for me—no one else is allowed to call me that—as he moves the knife in his hands, cutting the rope.

He brushes his blue hair back with a smoldering grin before lifting himself off the sand, swimming over to me.

"Need a hand with that?"

"We're fine, Merrick," Caspian says. "Go back to not paying attention to the rest of us."

"I didn't miss *that* much," he mutters.

"*Sure,*" Caspian replies.

Merrick gives him a mock-annoyed look, rolling his eyes as he grabs the net, helping us to untangle the rock.

"How did we get stuck on clean up duty?" Merrick asks, using his most charming voice as he sidles up next to me.

"We volunteered," I remind him.

"Mmm," he murmurs. "*You* volunteered. I just followed."

"Nothing new there, brother," Caspian teases loudly. "Always following my twin around no matter where she goes."

Caspian has *no idea* why Merrick and I spend so much time together.

"Shut up, Casp," Merrick chides, winking at me.

What neither of the boys knows is that I didn't volunteer just to help out—I'm on a mission.

"It amazes me how the humans are still so intent on capturing us," Caspian murmurs. "It's been a hundred years since Persephone ruined the alliance for us."

"Be fair, Casp—it wasn't *just* Persephone. Chantay was instrumental in all of this—most say she was the mastermind and her daughter just followed along."

My fingers work to cut away the net waving gently in the current. The knife in my hand is far more effective than the broken shells I sometimes resort to using for cutting up the instruments of death that fishermen leave in the ocean when they snag on something like coral or rocks.

"It's a shame we can't just sing this work away," Coralie swims over, attempting to carry a large, round ball. She barely manages to roll it across the sea floor.

"That's not the way sireny works, starfish," I correct her. "And stop playing with that canon ball."

My little sister pouts, looking up.

"I'm not playing with it, I'm trying to help," she mutters.

"We don't need to collect human things, just remove the dangerous ones," I remind her. Coralie has only been out to help us a few times, but I'd rather she stay at home —she's too young for me to be able to sneak off and run missions while she's with us, and Caspian will start to catch on if I dump her in his care all the time.

"It would still be easier if we could sing it away," she grumbles, running hair hands through her blonde hair.

"We are not sirens, Cor, and don't even suggest that," I snap. Caspian and Merrick stop to look at me. I try not to blush as I lower my voice. "We are not like that, Coralie. Sireny has been outlawed since great-great-grandmother Aila caught Persephone sirening the prince."

"We're better off," Caspian mumbles. "We don't need the humans to survive. They haven't been able to find us in a hundred years anyway, so who cares what stupid stunt Persephone and her mother pulled?"

"You mean *aside* from hundreds of dead humans, the mer population splitting, our entire kingdom having to leave our home and move here, and—*oh, yes*—the entire human race hunting us for a century?" I chide him.

"Settle down, children," Merrick chimes in, playfully trying to quell an impending argument.

This is why Caspian has never been informed of my extracurricular activities over the last few years. This is also why Merrick *has* been on most of my missions with me.

"Well, maybe we could train the sharks to move this stuff for us," Coralie suggests.

I certainly have my hands full with this one.

"Coralie, it's all we could do to train them to act as a barrier for Scylla, *for coral's sake*. It's not like they're pets —they don't have the ability to open things like an octopus does. They're there to eat—that's all."

"Well maybe grandma Aila should have come up with a better plan," Coralie mumbles.

"Aila saved us all, Cor," I eye her. "Show a little respect. She prevented Persephone from destroying the entire mer population. She even managed to bring Persephone in from the open seas."

I idolized my great-great-grandmother and aunts— they were heroes. Aila even saved the humans, though they didn't *deserve* her help one bit.

"Princess Kailania helped," Coralie persists. "So did Ebba. And Chantay went on to live and cause destruction for *years* before she died."

"Coralie," Merrick interrupts, flicking his hand to send a small seahorse toward her. "You understand the sirens terrorize the mer *and* the humans, right? Your ancestors did a great thing when they set up the shark barrier to prevent them from attacking us here in Scylla."

Coralie has always loved the stories of our great-great-grandmother and always wanted to visit the old kingdom, so she's just being stubborn because she doesn't want to work.

"I know," she sighs. My sister tries to suppress her

grin when the brown seahorse darts by her. "I just wish this were easier—or more fun."

"Tell you what," I smile, suddenly getting an idea. "Why don't you let Casp take you home and Merrick and I will finish up here. We're almost done anyway."

She cheers before my twin can protest. He grumbles, brushing back his hair.

"You two behave," he pretends to be serious, pointing at us. He wraps his arm protectively around our sister and guides her through the currents along the ocean floor.

When I turn back around, Merrick is working over-time to cut up the abandoned net. He nods for me to join him.

"I take it we have somewhere to be?" he asks casually.

"Yes."

"You weren't planning on taking me along, were you?" Merrick glances at me through his long, wavy bangs.

He caught me.

"It's not a big deal."

"Everything we do is a big deal, Celena. Every time we get near the shark barrier or swim up one of the reefs, it's a big deal."

"They wouldn't have trained us for this if they didn't want us to do it," I say, rolling my eyes at him.

"Just remember *which one of us* nearly swam into a

bloom of jellyfish last time we went out *alone*," he reminds me with a smirk.

"I only did that because you showed up and distracted me."

"You mispronounced *saved*." He grins wildly.

"Hardly, pretty boy."

We snap each rope on the net, making sure no mer or sea creature would get tangled in it. At least this one wasn't covered in barbs like the last one I found.

"I like your *iluse* today," Merrick adds, eyeing my chest covering. "Judging by those weapons you hid on it and called decorations, I'm guessing your little mission isn't as serene as you led me to believe."

Of course he'd notice the broken shells I hid in the netting and decor of my top—Merrick notices *everything*.

I slip my knife into the pouch tucked along my belt where it rests over my hips as my partner does the same. Belts were always traditionally worn by mermen a century ago to show power and prestige. The mermen would wear them specifically for special events or if they held a place of power. Now, most mer have a version they wear, especially when going to town or leaving the kingdom proper.

"So where are we going?" Merrick asks.

"This way," I reply, darting away.

I race around the seaweed gardens, swimming just

high enough that their wispy tips don't touch me as I glide over them. A sea turtle swims off to the left, not bothering to take notice of us.

"There's been word that the sirens have found a way in on the west side of the kingdom. I just want to check and make sure nothing has changed since we've last been there."

"Did they *ask* you to check?" Merrick challenges me.

"She doesn't have to," I snip, flicking my tail to propel me faster, leaving Merrick in a trail of bubbles.

"*She* the queen or *she* your mother?" He easily catches up to me, having a far more powerful tail than I do.

"Take your pick," I retort.

"It's rough being princess to the entire mer kingdom, isn't it?" Merrick mocks.

"I'm barely a princess," I remind him, darting around a school of fish. Merrick pulls away at the last second, barely missing them as I smirk.

"You descend from royalty. Just because your cousin holds the official crown, doesn't make you any less of a princess."

"I'm a warrior, Merrick. I hardly sit around the palace all day."

"Neither does your cousin," he points out as we slow our pace. "You all work for this kingdom. *You* just take it more seriously than the rest."

"Aila did."

"You don't have to do everything Princess Aila did," he counters. "And if you'll recall, she didn't set out to do any of that—it just happened.

"Next thing I know, you'll be swimming to the surface to meet some human prince." He rolls his eyes at me as he brings up Prince Jarek, the human Persephone tried to siren when she caused the war.

"I have no intention of befriending a human, thank you very much. That would be a stroke in the wrong direction for sure."

"Ah, but speaking of a stroke in the *right* direction, looks like our rides just arrived," Merrick calls, rushing forward. His hand darts out, catching hold of a dolphin.

He quickly reaches back, grabbing my hand as the creature pulls us forward. Once he pulls me to him, I catch my own ride.

The coral barrier stretches up high toward the surface of the ocean, protecting Scylla from intruders. The barrier blocks larger ships from entering most of the territory, protecting us from many of the humans' attempts to find us.

While their searches have slowed, it's very clear that they are not done looking for trophies to take home. A year ago, I found a book that had fallen to the ocean floor describing the most absurd ideas the humans had about mer. One page detailed our bone structure—which, in fact, they *do* know from cutting up our ancestors—while another page contained information about how we cry pearls and dissolve into foam when we have our hearts broken.

Humans are curious creatures who *clearly* haven't learned much in the last two centuries.

When we finally let go of the dolphins, Merrick and I examine the coral. Nothing looks out of place, though it's been months since I was last here. I only make it out to this side of the kingdom a few times a year, just to check on it. We have mermen standing watch at all times, but I like to see it for myself.

"What I don't understand is how the sirens have been getting in," Merrick murmurs. "We have all of these barriers in place—we're protected. How are they slipping in?"

"We've only seen evidence of a few so far—barely enough to warn the people."

"We've never officially found any inside Scylla, I know." Merrick sighs. "But *how* is this possible?"

The few sirens we've noticed have disappeared before we could bring them in for questioning—the mer have only seen them from a distance.

Rumors have spread like seaweed that the sirens have changed in appearance—long, hideous noses, scraggly hair, and sea serpent-like tails.

I know that can't be true based on the books I've found from the humans. Sirens still look just like the mer—because they still *are* mer. They just cultivated their wicked talents while the mer forced it out of our offspring.

Once, we all had the ability to sing a human into doing our bidding. Now, only sirens hold that dark magic. Instead, we avoid humans and their destruction, leaving us no need for the deadly songs sirens have the ability to sing.

True, Marcelline—*the defender of the sea*—originally sirened King Leon into creating an agreement with the mer, but that only lasted a century until Persephone ruined that promise of safety for us. Marcelline's great-great-granddaughter, Aila, tried desperately to save the agreement and repair our relationship with the humans, but today we find ourselves living deep under the sea, refusing to venture to the surface where we once used our voices to save humans on the rough ocean surface.

Now, we wouldn't surface to save a drowning fisherman or guide a ship safely through a storm for any price. We don't associate with the population trying to murder us.

"Can you feel that?" Merrick asks, holding his arms out to his side. "The tide is changing. Just beyond the coral reef, the temperature drops. It's not a terrible difference, but just enough to be noticeably cooler."

I pause, giving Merrick his moment. Truthfully, I can sense the difference as the water drifts around me.

"I still don't see anything different," I finally announce.

"I don't either." He frowns. "We should go. We'll come up with another idea."

Instead of turning around with him, I flip my tail, propelling myself toward the surface. A moment later, Merrick is by my side, grumbling.

Careful not to touch the coral to avoid damaging it, I peer over the top of it, looking out into the blue ocean. Seaweed waves against the current while small fish swim in and out of the grass.

A shadow passes over the sea floor, stealthily gliding over rocks, sand, and seahorses. I gasp.

"Get down," Merrick commands, pulling me down below the top of the coral. I struggled to get away.

"No," I protest, prying his fingers off my waist. "We need to see the ship."

Reluctantly, he swims us both back up to the edge.

The ship drops a net that silently slices through the water. Fish dart out of the way as the fishermen search for dinner—or a mer trophy to string up on their mast before taking them back to land to show their people.

We watch as the net drags through the ocean, something shiny sparkling from the ropes. Suddenly, a figure darts out from behind the coral on the ground. She races toward the net, swimming as quickly as she can.

"What is she doing?" Merrick whispers as the mermaid catches up to the net.

The mermaid suddenly changes course, propelling herself straight up to the middle of the net. She tries untangling the shiny object from the rope. When she can't free it, she struggles against it, pulling as hard as she can to rip the object free.

It's hard to see her from so far away as she thrusts her hands deeper into the net, frantically trying to retrieve the object. After a moment, her movements change as anger and frustration shift to panic.

"She's stuck," I murmur.

"Celena," Merrick quickly warns, looking at me. "We can't."

"We can't let them take her," I plead with him.

"She's a siren. King Gaspar made it very clear we aren't allowed to help them."

"King Gaspar has been dead for nearly a century," I protest. "Even so, he did everything in his power to try to keep us all together."

"You realize that only one of us gets forgiveness if we decide to become a rebel, right?" Merrick remarks, giving me a look before glancing at the mermaid. The net lifts toward the surface and his face falls.

"Merrick," I shout. My worry was in vain—Merrick was already swimming over the reef.

I flick my tail, racing forward to follow him as we rush toward the siren. No matter how hard we try, we'll never reach her in time.

The last thing I see is her red tail lifting out of the water, her wrist still tangled in the net as she screams. Merrick never slows, pushing to reach her.

"Merrick!" My shouts don't deter him. He doesn't stop until she's gone. My friend pauses in the water, floating in the bubbles that trailed off of the mermaid's thrashing tail.

"We have to go." His voice is dark when he turns back to me. I stare at the bottom of the boat, far closer than it should be. "Len, *we have to go.*"

As quickly as a dolphin, Merrick dives at me, knocking me out of my trance. He pushes me back, tail beating against the water to move us away from the boat and out of siren territory.

"Merrick, we can't leave her."

"Oh, yes, we can," he says as if it's not an option. "I wasn't joking about this grace thing—we crossed a line just now. As a royal, you might be given leniency, but I certainly will not."

"Our mothers worked together, Merrick—you'll be fine."

Something sparkles above us, reflecting off the water.

Red trickles down, slowly fading to where the sky meets the sea.

A firework—a celebration of a mermaid catch.

"Right now, they're tying that mermaid to the beams on their ship, Celena. I won't have them do that to you—we're leaving."

"Merrick, she's a mermaid. She's about to suffer the unthinkable. Maybe we can rescue her."

"You know that's been attempted before and hasn't worked," he argues. He's terrified for my safety and while I understand that, I can't just swim away.

"None of those mer know as much about humans as you and I do—we've studied them," I reply.

"From books. We've studied them *from books.*" He looks desperate, pleading with me to turn back.

"We have to," I whisper.

"Len," he whispers back. His fingers grip the shell necklace that rests on his chest. When he sighs, I know I've won.

He grabs my hand as we race after the boat. The water rushes against my ears, flooding my senses. We push harder, forcing ourselves beyond what any mer is normally capable of doing.

My hand slips to the knife on my hip. I fumble for it, unable to detach it as I swim toward the human boat—I doubt it would do any good, even if we *could* reach them.

"Stay below the surface," Merrick warns, grasping my hand tighter.

Bits of my pink hair float around me as we come to a sudden halt. We're far enough away from the boat that the men likely won't take notice of us, but close enough that I can see them trying to tie the thrashing mermaid to the mast of their ship. She struggles against them, trying to siren them into submission.

Her singing appears to be working as most of the men back away. Several untie her as she frantically sings. I'm mesmerized by her ability to control them.

"I didn't think that was possible," I murmur.

I know that we once all had the ability to control humans with our voices, but over the last century, that skill was taken away from us, trained out of our people until it no longer existed. To see sireny so strong was an incredible experience—I almost wish I could surface and listen to her song.

They pass her along the deck of the ship near the edge, close enough that we can see her moving. Not everyone is under her spell though—several men race toward her in anger.

The edge of the ship covers our view. Merrick holds me back. In my distraction, I had nearly surfaced to see the scene unfold.

"We can help her if she makes it into the water, but

Len, we have to be careful. Your mother will kill me if you get hurt."

"You're more scared of my mother than you are of the queen," I snap back.

When the mermaid crashes into the ocean, red plumes around her, mimicking the color of her tail.

Read the rest by grabbing your copy of The Siren Wars at sirenwarsinfo.kmrobinsonbooks.com

BONUS SCENES

Want to read a bonus scene from The Siren Wars? We're giving out an exclusive bonus scene over on the K.M. Robinson Facebook page!

Get it by sending the page a direct message at facebook.com/kmrobinsonbooks

We're also giving away Siren Wars freebies in the newsletter. Join for free books, excerpts, and more! newsletter.kmrobinsonbooks.com

We're constantly giving out additional bonus scenes for preorder swag, giveaways, and more, so watch the social media pages carefully for the next scene giveaway.

WORLD PORTALS

BONUS FACEBOOK FILTERS

Want to get your hands on some incredible Facebook filters for Siren Wars? Now you have the ability to get filters for the story, characters, etc right inside your phone.

You can use these on your photos, profile pictures, videos, and live broadcasts. All you have to do is like my author page and they will automatically show up in your filters!

I've even taken these clips and put them on Instagram Stories by saving them to my phone and uploading them to Instagram.

Visit www.facebook.com/kmrobinsonbooks to grab these filters for your photos, videos, and broadcasts! Bonus points for tagging me @kmrobinsonbooks so I can see how you're supporting The Siren Wars.

ABOUT THE AUTHOR

K.M. Robinson is a storyteller who creates new worlds both in her writing and in her fine arts conceptual photography. She is a marketing, branding and social media strategy educator who is recognized at first sight by her very long hair. She is a creative who focuses on photography, videography, couture dress making, and writing to express the stories she needs to tell. She almost always has a camera within reach. Visit her at her website: www.kmrobinsonbooks.com

CONNECT ON SOCIAL MEDIA

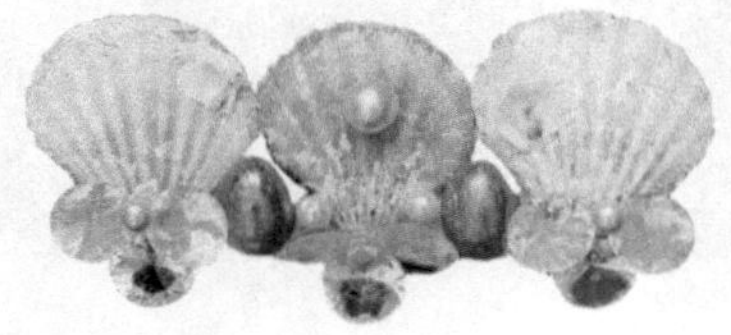

facebook.com/kmrobinsonbooks

instagram.com/kmrobinsonbooks

twitter.com/kmrobinsonbooks

Get free books and excerpts of other K.M. Robinson
books at excerpt.kmrobinsonbooks.com

ALSO BY K.M. ROBINSON

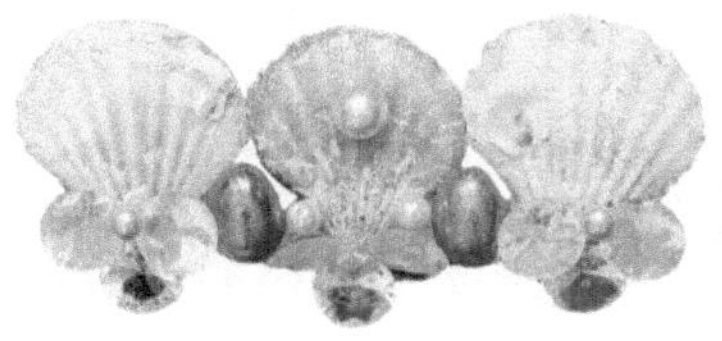

The Siren Wars Saga

Book One: The Siren Wars

Book Two: Darker Depths

Book Three: Beyond The Shores

Origins of the Siren Wars: Prequel Novella

The Jaded Duology

Book One: Jaded

Book Two: Risen

The Complete Series Boxset/Omnibus with exclusive epilogue
(Summer 2018)

The Golden Trilogy

Book One: Golden

Forged: A Golden Novella

Book Two: Locked

Book Three: Edge

The Complete Series Boxset/Omnibus with exclusive bonus novella, Tempered

The Legends Chronicles

Along Came A Spider: A Prequel Novelette

And They'll Come Home: A Prequel Novelette

The Revolution of Jack Frost (Coming November 2018)

Virtually Sleeping Beauty: A Novella Retelling

The Goose Girl and The Artificial: A Novella Retelling

The Sinking: A Novella Retelling

JADED: BOOK ONE OF THE JADED DUOLOGY

Her father failed in his mission to take control from the Commander, a defeat that has cost Jade her life. She will die as punishment. Now she belongs to the Commander's son—as his wife. Knowing his intent is to quietly kill her in revenge, Jade's every move is calculated to survive—until she learns her death ensures the safety of her father and her entire town.

Roan doesn't want to kill Jade, but once his family isolates her from her father and community, his only choice is to go through with the plan. Jade doesn't make it easy as she tries to sway him into falling for her. Each misstep makes him question his cause. Each moment makes every decision harder, but the Commander won't allow him to fail.

One chooses life. One chooses death. In the midst of the chaos, only one will succeed.

Now available!
Learn more about The Jaded Duology at
jadedinfo.kmrobinsonbooks.com

GOLDEN: BOOK ONE OF THE GOLDEN TRILOGY

Goldilocks was never naive. She was sent on a mission and Dov Baer is her new target.

When the girl with the golden hair betrays everyone, not even she has hope of surviving.

The stories say that Goldilocks was a naïve girl who wandered into a house one day. Those stories were wrong. She was never naïve. It was all a perfectly executed plan to get her into the Baers' group to destroy them.

Trained by her cousin, Lowell, and handler, Shadoe, Auluria's mission is to destroy the Baers by getting close to the youngest brother, Dov, his brother and sister-in-law and the leaders of the Baers' group.

When she realizes Dov isn't as evil as her cousin led her to believe, she must figure out how to play both sides or her deception will cause everyone in her world to burn.

If her allegiances are discovered, either side could destroy her...if the Society doesn't get her first.

Available now!

Learn more about The Golden Trilogy at

goldeninfo.kmrobinsonbooks.com

ALONG CAME A SPIDER: THE FIRST PREQUEL NOVELETTE TO THE LEGENDS CHRONICLES

Little Hacker Muffet
sat on her tuffet
destroying her cords and Way.
Along came a hacker named Spider,
who sat down beside her
and frightened his opponent away.

WHEN FET, ONE OF THE MOST SKILLED HACKERS IN THE Legends, discovers her best friend and leader of her group has been abducted and held for ransom, she must escape unnoticed and find Peep before it's too late.

When Spider, a new recruit training to join her hacker ring, slips out with her and claims to have a plan to save her friend, Fet is forced to bring him along. As she discovers he's not who he claims to be, she faces grave danger and learns just how deadly a spider bite can be.

Now available!
Learn more about The Legends Chronicles at
acasinfo.kmrobinsonbooks.com

VIRTUALLY SLEEPING BEAUTY

She may be doing battle in the virtual world, but in the real world, they can't wake her up…

All Rora wants is to help people as class president, give her time to local charities, and quietly earn her way to the top level of the virtual reality system that the entire country uses without anyone noticing she's the second best player in the game.

All Royce wants to do is level up as a knight inside the gaming system, slay dragons, and eventually play his way to controlling the palace as he takes the crown away from the reigning queen.

When his Aunt Perry calls him, hysterically screaming that her goddaughter, Rora, has been inside for more than the four hours the game allows, Royce rushes over to help.

Entering the game, Royce soon discovers that Rora is trapped inside the system after an encounter with an evil magician who can change forms inside the game and control the virtual world. If he and his friend can't help her beat the game, she might not be able to wake up in the real world at all.

When virtual knights and princesses meet to slay dragons and defeat evil rulers, there's nothing stopping them from suffering real-world consequences too.

To wake her up, he must enter the game and help her beat it.

Now available!
Learn more about Virtually Sleeping Beauty at
vsbinfo.kmrobinsonbooks.com

www.ingramcontent.com/pod-product-compliance
Lightning Source LLC
Chambersburg PA
CBHW032021180726
48283CB00008B/2785